# THE POCKET

# Sherlock Holmes

Quizzes & Puzzles

Published in 2024
by Gemini Adult Books Ltd
Part of Gemini Books Group

Based in Woodbridge and London
Marine House, Tide Mill Way
Woodbridge, Suffolk IP12 1AP
United Kingdom

www.geminibooks.com

Text and Design © 2024 Gemini Books Group
Part of the Gemini Pocket series

Cover image: thegraphicsfairy.com

ISBN 978-1-91708-293-8

Printed in China

10 9 8 7 6 5 4 3 2 1

MIX
Paper | Supporting
responsible forestry
FSC® C008047

# THE
# POCKET

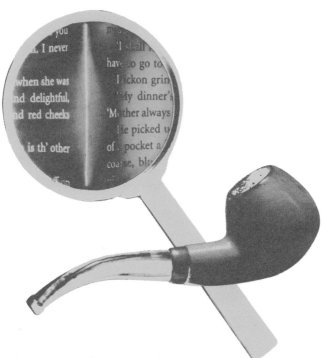

# Sherlock
# Holmes

Quizzes & Puzzles

**G:**

# Contents

# INTRODUCTION

The Game is Afoot! Here is a compendium of intriguing puzzles and quizzes to test your knowledge of the cases that so fascinated the world when reported by Dr John Watson in the pages of *The Strand Magazine* and elsewhere.

Holmes was a secretive man, but he did let slip a few details of his private life, which you may remember. For the most part, he struggled to understand women, but there were certainly some he did admire, not least the formidable Irene Adler. There are questions about his many adversaries and the cases that he solved – also the very few that defeated him.

There are crossword puzzles based on Watson's reports of Holmes's cases, laced with a few cryptic clues. Puzzle grids lead you through the foggy streets of Holmes's London and out into the countryside, hot on the trail of the master detective and his sidekick. Anagrams further test your ingenuity and there is a maze to trap the unwary.

Throughout the book, Sherlock Holmes's short story titles are rendered in the Dancing Men cipher, inspired by 'The Adventure of the Dancing Men', where Holmes realizes the figures form a substitution cipher. Each figure represents a letter of the alphabet, and a flag indicates the end of a word.

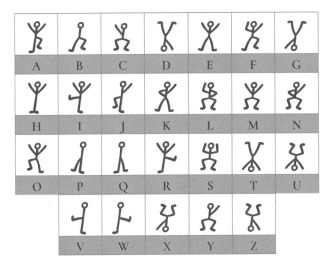

Conan Doyle used eighteen symbols, excluding F, J, K, Q, U, W, X and Z. The symbols for P and V were similar. Above is a code in alphabetical order. Finally, there is a quiz to test your knowledge of Holmes's creator, Sir Arthur Conan Doyle.

Explanations as to how to solve the quizzes and other puzzles and all the answers can be found at the back of the book.

# SHERLOCK HOLMES
# by Arthur Conan Doyle

The fictional character of the super sleuth Sherlock Holmes was cleverly invented by the writer and physician Arthur Conan Doyle in *A Study in Scarlet*, published in *Beeton's Christmas Annual* of 1887. The first collection of the Holmes's detective stories, published as *The Adventures of Sherlock Holmes*, appeared in 1892. In total, there were four novels and fifty-six short stories, a body of work that contributed to the creation of modern crime fiction.

Born in Edinburgh, Scotland, on 22 May 1859, Doyle was sent to England to school at the age of nine, before being educated in Austria (1875–6). After receiving a Bachelor of Medicine and Master of Surgery degrees from the University of Edinburgh, he was a ship's surgeon and had his own practice in Portsmouth, dividing himself between medicine and writing. He died of a heart attack on 7 July 1930.

As to Holmes himself, he is said to be based on Doyle's professor at the University of Edinburgh Medical School, Dr Joseph Bell, and possesses almost supernatural skills of observation and deduction. His backstory is only slowly revealed over the course of the stories. He shares his home at 221B Baker Street, London, with his housekeeper, Mrs Hudson. He suffers from bipolar disorder, habitually smokes a pipe and plays a violin. Incidentally, the meerschaum pipe and deerstalker hat that became forever associated with the character were not in the literature at all, but first employed by the earliest actor to have portrayed the role, William Gillette, at the turn of the twentieth century.

## 'Work is the best antidote to sorrow, my dear Watson.'

*The Adventure of the Empty House*

The Second Stain

The Solitary Cyclist

The Dancing Men

The Hound of the Baskervilles

The Speckled Band

The Reigate Squire

The Boscombe Valley Mystery

The Red-Headed League

The Norwood Builder

The Abbey Grange

The Final Problem

The Bruce-Partington Plans

# Quizzes
# & Puzzles

# First Things First

Can you give the first names of the following characters who appear in the four long stories: *A Study in Scarlet*, *The Sign of the Four*, *The Hound of the Baskervilles* and *The Valley of Fear*?

1  GREGSON – the smartest of the Scotland Yarders

2  CHARPENTIER – sub-lieutenant in Her Majesty's Navy

3  FERRIER – adopted in the desert

4  MORAN – chief of staff to the Napoleon of crime

5  BALDWIN – boss of the Scowrers

6  SHAFTER – boarding-house keeper

7  MARVIN – captain of Mine Police

8  STAPLETON – wife or sister of a naturalist

9  MAJOR SHOLTO – friend of Captain Morstan

10  JONES – investigator of the death of Bartholomew, brother of Thaddeus

11  DREBNER – found dead at Lauriston Gardens

12  PORLOCK – so-called

# Dancing Men Cipher Puzzle 1

Decode the Dancing Men cipher below to discover the title of a Sherlock Holmes short story. See pages 6–7 for more information on the Dancing Men cipher.

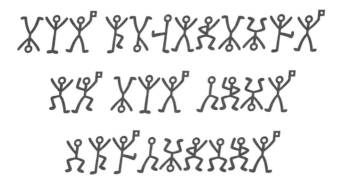

# Street Walker

This puzzle conceals nine streets, roads, etc. (but not towns) mentioned in the four long stories. First find Baker Street, then trace your way from there. Each word follows a straight line, which may read horizontally, vertically or diagonally, backwards or forwards. The next word always starts from a position that is immediately adjacent to the last letter used. A letter may be used more than once, or not at all. All the names consist of more than one word.

```
K C E C A R R E T Y E B
H R H O L L A N D A L A
A S A E V O R G G U K T
L T P L A C E N O Q U E
L H N W E Y C O U R T M
L G B A K E R S O O W A
A I A L G L S S I T N Y
N N T L M D T B L I E F
E K X E V U R A M W C I
S T O Y B A E K N O A E
S Q U A R E E Y E T L L
T E K R A M T O P O P D
```

# Crossword 1

This crossword is based on *The Hound of the Baskervilles*. Non-cryptic clues, which are the names of characters or places mentioned in the story or a quotation from the recorded sayings of Holmes, are marked with an asterisk.

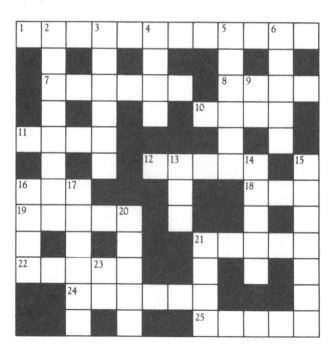

## Across

1,2 Initialled on a stick. (7,5,8)*
7 He was hounded to death. (6)*
8 Foolish person to arrange a toga thus. (4)
10 'A man of precise ..., evidently.' (4)*
11 After 15, here 'a false step means death.' (4)*
12 See 22 across.*
16 An apt arrangement for a peg. (3)
18 A peak that may be Black or Cleft. (3)*
19 See 13 down.*
21 Palindromic lady. (5)
22,12 The postscript of her letter was rescued from the ashes. (5,5) *
24 Beryl ..., a beauty from Costa Rica. (6)*
25 Where 'the brown earth becomes ruddy'. (5)*

For Down clues, please turn over.

## Down

2    See 1 across.*
3    Assistance with a solid art form. (6)
4    Want Eden like this. (4)
5    '[I]nto the ... where we balance probabilities and choose the most likely.' (6)*
6    Is it disreputable to be sheltered from the sun? (5)
9    Two-thirds of a ton. (2)
13,19  Place of a regular nocturnal walk. (3,5)*
14   'A ... of family portraits is enough to convert a man to the doctrine of reincarnation.' (5)*
15   Hamlet where 'an M.R.C.S. had his H.Q.' (7)*
16   Remarkable in that all is revealed. (4)
17   All assist when they put their hands to this. (6)
20   'For ... he had been a desperate and dangerous man.' (5)*
21   A drink that could be made differently. (4)
23   A god raps without a further thought. (2)

# Dancing Men Cipher Puzzle 2

Decode the Dancing Men cipher below to discover the title of a Sherlock Holmes short story. See pages 6–7 for more information on the Dancing Men cipher.

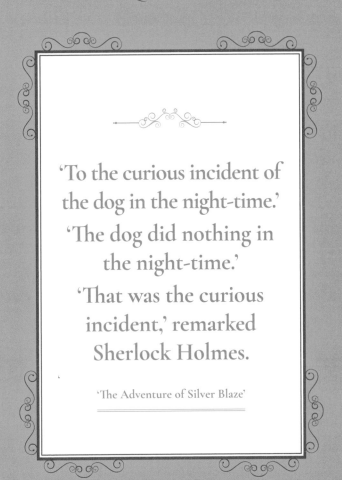

'To the curious incident of the dog in the night-time.'
'The dog did nothing in the night-time.'
'That was the curious incident,' remarked Sherlock Holmes.

'The Adventure of Silver Blaze'

# Holmes in Disguise

Watson asserted that he became accustomed 'to my friend's amazing powers in the use of disguises'. He nevertheless was often fooled by Holmes. Can you say which cases Holmes was engaged in when he disguised himself as the following:

1   An amiable and simple-minded Non-conformist clergyman?

2   An aged man, clad in seafaring garb, with an old pea-jacket buttoned up to this throat?

3   An old man, very thin, very wrinkled, with an opium pipe dangling between his knees?

4   A venerable Italian priest?

5   An old book collector with sharp, wizened face and a frame of white hair?

6   A rakish young workman, with a goatee beard, a swagger and a clay pipe?

7   An unshaven French workman in a blue blouse, with a cudgel in his hand?

8   A motor expert?

9   An old lady?

10   A drunken-looking groom, ill-kept and side-whiskered?

# Dancing Men Cipher Puzzle 3

Decode the Dancing Men cipher below to discover the title of a Sherlock Holmes short story. See pages 6–7 for more information on the Dancing Men cipher.

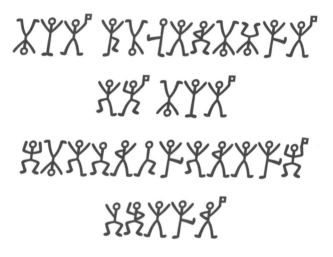

# Pub Crawl

When their investigations took them out of London, it was customary for Holmes and Watson to seek comfortable quarters at country pubs and hotels.

Can you answer the following questions regarding hostelries?

1 Where in Ross did Holmes find an exceptionally comfortable sofa?

2 What did Holmes and Watson wait to observe at the window of the Crown Inn, Stoke Moran?

3 Whom did Holmes and Watson meet at the Black Swan Hotel, Winchester?

4 What missing person did Holmes find at the Fighting Cock Inn?

5 What did Holmes advertise as having been found near the White Hart Tavern?

6 What case was Holmes engaged upon when he stayed at the Brambletye Hotel, Forest Row?

7 Why did a police constable desert his post to go to the Ivy Plant?

8 What singular experience led Holmes and Watson to take quarters at the Bull Inn, Esher?

9 At the Chequers, Camford, what did Holmes consider to be (a) above mediocrity, and (b) above reproach?

10 What 'mixture of the modern and the mediaeval' took Holmes and Watson to the Chequers, Lamberley?

11 In 'The Adventure of Shoscombe Old Place', what did Holmes and Watson pose as while staying at the Green Dragon?

12 Watson shared quarters at the Railway Arms, Little Purlington, with a murderer. Who was he?

# Title Search

The titles of fifteen Sherlock Holmes short stories are hidden in the grid. Each title consists of more than one word, but the words 'a', 'an', 'the' and 'adventure of' have been omitted. Each word follows a straight line, and the next word in that title commences from a square immediately adjacent to the last letter used, but may run in a different direction. Words may run forwards, backwards, upwards or downwards, but not diagonally. A letter may be used more than once or not at all.

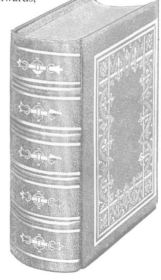

```
S U O I R T S U L L I B L E R
C A S M A P Q L S U N O B L E
L I C I M G N I P E E R C B G
I R O N A D C O E F F H W A D
E O T L N Y A N C R T Y U C O
N L T C N T R S K O D T G H L
T G Y Y A A D M L V E I L E D
X I R C V E B A E H J T M L N
E T A L A R O N D B A N D O T
L S T I L T A E Y W L E F R O
Z W I S T E R I A L Z D B J O
Z Z L T N B D P E O F I R D F
U P O L K O C T S D E V I L S
P I S M G X T E A G F I R E D
E T A G I E R K C E L C R I C
```

# A Study in Scarlet

Written in 1887, the plot revolves around a body found in Brixton, London, with the word 'Rache' written on the wall in blood. Sherlock and Watson team up to investigate a series of murders that lead to a remote house in the English countryside.

'There's the scarlet thread of murder running through the colourless skein of life, and our duty is to unravel it, and isolate it, and expose every inch of it.'

*A Study in Scarlet*

# Crossword 2

This crossword puzzle is based on *The Valley of Fear*. Non-cryptic clues, which are the names of characters or places mentioned in the story or a quotation from the recorded sayings of Holmes, are marked with an asterisk.

.

**Across**

2   See 18 across.*

5   'A ..., Watson ... a great, big, thumping, obtrusive, uncompromising ...'
    (3)*

7   'I can hardly recall any case where the features have been more ...' (8)*

9,17  Edited by James Stranger. (5, 6)*

10   Commercial Hotel at Tunbridge Wells. (5)*

11   Strike who quietly? (4)

15   Turfs are a little odd in a ship. (4)

17   See 9 across.*

18,2  Alias John McMurdo. (5,7)*

19   'The temptation to form premature theories upon insufficient ... is
    the bane of our profession.' (4)*

20   Different heads err to make stickers. (8)

24   See 19 down.*

25   Black Jack (7)*

For Down clues please turn over.

35

## Down

1, 4   'There are many ... which I could ... as easily as I do the
       apocrypha of the agony column.' (7,4)*

3      Baldwin died in his place. (7)*

4      See 1 down.*

6      Wife of 3. (3)*

8      'As I focus my mind upon it, it seems ... less impenetrable.' (6)*

11     'It is a clumsy fabrication ... simply could not be true.' (5)*

12     Demand an arrangement. (5)

13     Why follow father to settle a debt? (3)

14     'The interplay of ... and the oblique uses of knowledge are often
       of extraordinary interest.' (5)*

16     Let Ida play a small part.

19,24  'Is it possible that you have not penetrated the fact that the
       case hangs upon the missing ... - ...?' (4-4)*

21     Hold back a mother. (3)

22     It may precede or follow a biped. (3)

23     Pitch back the rodent.

# Dancing Men Cipher Puzzle 4

Decode the Dancing Men cipher below to discover the title of a Sherlock Holmes short story. See pages 6–7 for more information on the Dancing Men cipher.

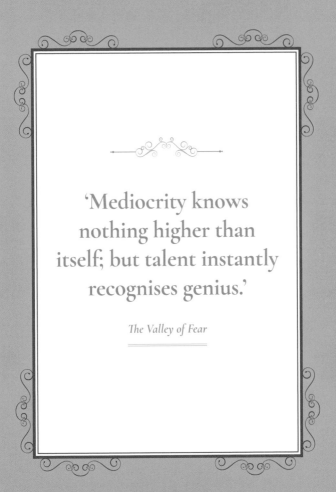

'Mediocrity knows
nothing higher than
itself; but talent instantly
recognises genius.'

*The Valley of Fear*

# Read All About It

Holmes's files contained an impressive collection of newspaper cuttings. Can you answer the following questions regarding newspapers mentioned in Holmes's cases?

1   Where were Holmes and Watson when they read in the *Telegraph* of the disappearance of Silver Blaze?

2   What did Arthur Pinner read in the *Evening Standard* that led him to attempt suicide?

3   For what purpose did Miss Mary Sutherland place an advertisement in the *Chronicle*?

4   An account of whose death did Holmes read in the *Devon County Chronicle*?

5   What did Jabez Wilson see in the *Morning Chronicle* that led him to leave his pawnbroker's shop?

6   Whom did Holmes trap with an advertisement in the agony column of the *Daily Telegraph* in the Bruce-Partington case?

7   Whose murder at Pondicherry Lodge, Upper Norwood, was reported in the *Evening Standard*?

8   A *Daily Telegraph* report upon a sinister inscription on a wall referred to which case of Holmes?

9  What did the *Daily Chronicle* report was in a cardboard box received through the post by Miss Susan Cushing?

10 Why did Mrs Emilia Lucca, in the Red Circle case, have the *Daily Gazette* left outside her room every morning?

11 What did a paragraph in the *Morning Post Chronicle* announce concerning Violet de Merville in the Illustrious Client case?

12 In what case did the *North Surrey Observer* report that the smell of paint concealed that of gas?

# Murder

Can you pair the victim, in the left-hand column, with the appropriate killer from the right-hand column?

| | | | |
|---|---|---|---|
| 1 | Sir Eustace Brackenstall | A | Josiah Amberley |
| 2 | Richard Brunton | B | Jim Browner |
| 3 | Ray Ernest | C | Capt James Calhoun |
| 4 | Alec Fairbairn | D | Jack Crocker |
| 5 | Aloysius Garcia | E | Mme Henri Fournaye |
| 6 | Herr Heidegger | F | Reuben Hayes |
| 7 | Eduardo Lucas | G | Rachel Howells |
| 8 | John Openshaw | H | Leonardo |
| 9 | Mr Ronder | I | Don Juan Murillo |
| 10 | Victor Savage | J | Hugo Oberstein |
| 11 | Julia Stoner | K | Dr Grimesby Roylott |
| 12 | Arthur Cadogan West | L | Culverton Smith |

# Dancing Men Cipher Puzzle 5

Decode the Dancing Men cipher below to discover the title of a Sherlock Holmes short story. See pages 6–7 for more information on the Dancing Men cipher.

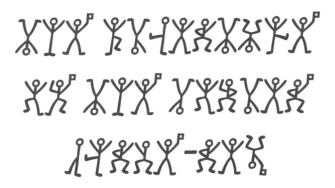

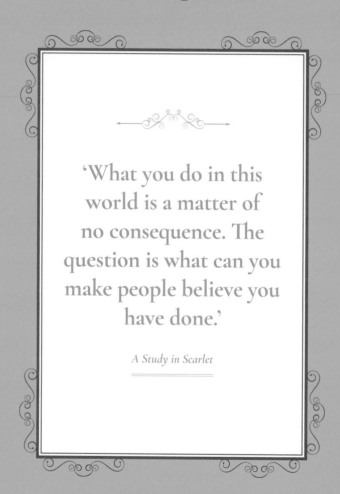

'What you do in this world is a matter of no consequence. The question is what can you make people believe you have done.'

*A Study in Scarlet*

# Holmes, the Man

Few details were recorded by Watson of Holmes's private life. Indeed, it is unlikely that Holmes confided many to the doctor. What then do you know of the following:

1   Who was the notable person with whom a grandmother of Holmes was connected?

2   Where was Holmes working when he was first introduced to Watson?

3   What did Holmes claim his knowledge of literature to be?

4   Who was the only friend Holmes made during his years at college?

5   What was Holmes's connection with Montague Street 'just around the corner from the British Museum'?

6   From whom did Holmes purchase a Stradivarius and at what price?

7   What, according to Watson, was Holmes's favourite weapon?

8   What was it about Holmes's revolver that upset Mrs Hudson?

9   What did Holmes keep in the coal-scuttle in his rooms at Baker Street?

10  Who gave Holmes an emerald tie-pin?

11  What graced the yard behind 221B Baker Street?

12  Which was the club of Holmes's brother, Mycroft?

# Dancing Men Cipher Puzzle 6

Decode the Dancing Men cipher below to discover the title of a Sherlock Holmes short story. See pages 6–7 for more information on the Dancing Men cipher.

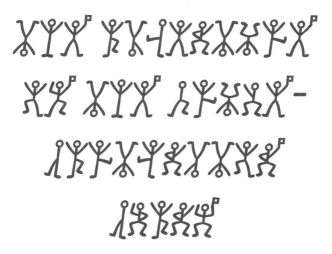

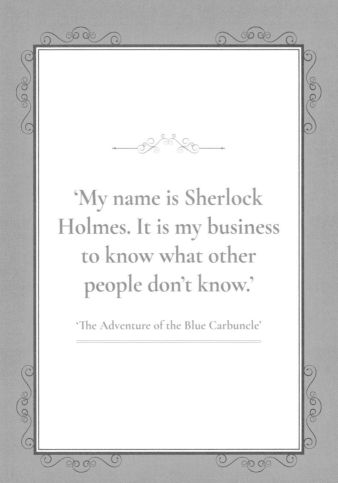

'My name is Sherlock
Holmes. It is my business
to know what other
people don't know.'

'The Adventure of the Blue Carbuncle'

# Crossword 3

This crossword puzzle is based on the short stories. Non-cryptic clues, which are the names of characters or places mentioned in the story or a quotation from the recorded sayings of Holmes, are marked with an asterisk.

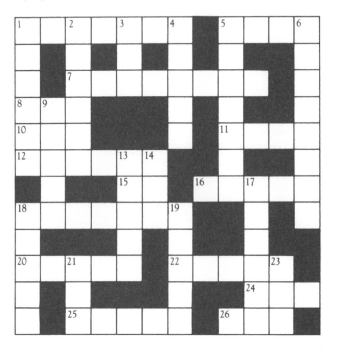

**Across**

1   The stockbroker's clerk. (7)*

5   See 13 down.*

7   Snake-catcher in the Crooked Man case. (8)*

8   First name of Hunter in the Silver Blaze case. (3)*

10  Nearly get even with the girl. (3)

11  *Little by Little* rice is mixed. (4)

12,22 Card player murdered by Colonel Moran (6,5)*

15  In short, that is. (2)

16  Holmes claimed to have been familiar with forty-two different impressions of these. (5)*

18  'Education never ends, Watson. It is a series of ... with the greatest for the last.' (7)*

20  Shoots forth the tapering folds. (5)

22  See 12 across.*

24  A note lacking direction becomes negative. (3)

25  Students or Gables. (5)*

26,19 'I trust that ... doth not wither nor custom ... my infinite variety.' (3,5)*

For Down clues please turn over.

## Down

1   Arthur and Harry, one and the same in the Stockbroker's Clerk case. (6)*
2   The Empty House opposite No. 221B. (6)*
3   Now change and confess. (3)
4   'I cannot agree with ... who rank modesty among the virtues.' (5)*
5   'I am accustomed to have ... at one end of my cases, but to have it at both ends is too confusing.' (7)*
6   'Your fatal habit of looking at everything from the point of view of a story instead of as a scientific ...' (8)*
9   Call out, or revoke without a king or queen. (5)
13, 5   *Cyanea capillata*, killer from the sea. (5,4)*
14   The lair eight returned to. (3)
17   'To let the brain work without sufficient material is like ... an engine.' (6)*
18   Vernon, Torrington or Wisteria. (5)*
19   See 26 across.*
21   Holmes smelled many a one in his investigations. (3)
23   Deer or eastern arrangement of fish eggs. (3)

# Dancing Men Cipher Puzzle 7

Decode the Dancing Men cipher below to discover the title of a Sherlock Holmes short story. See pages 6–7 for more information on the Dancing Men cipher.

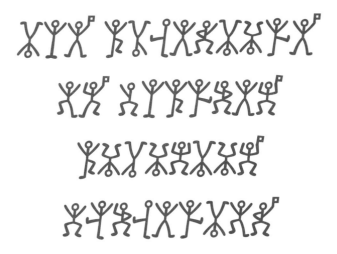

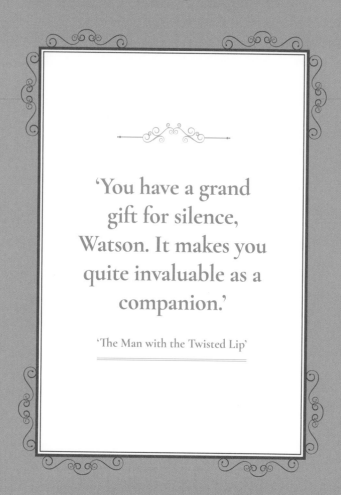

'You have a grand
gift for silence,
Watson. It makes you
quite invaluable as a
companion.'

'The Man with the Twisted Lip'

# Going to the Dogs

**A bull terrier 'freezing onto his ankle' leads to Holmes's 'first case'.**

1   What was that case? 'Man's best friend' figured in many of Holmes's other adventures. Do you know ...

2   ... by what means dog Toby followed the trail of Wooden-leg in *The Sign of the Four*?

3   ... how Holmes hastened the end of a terrier in *A Study in Scarlet*?

4   ... why the wolfhound, Roy, attacked Professor Presbury?

5   ... what means Holmes adopted to ensure that Pompey would be able to follow a doctor's carriage in the Missing Three-Quarter case?

6   ... why a spaniel barked furiously at a carriage leaving the gates of Shoscombe Old Place?

7   ... what other dog, besides 'the coal black hound' is mentioned in *The Hound of the Baskervilles*?

8   ... how a dog died in the Sussex Vampire case?

9   ... what was curious about the behaviour of a dog in the night-time at King's Pyland?

10  ... what animal was killed by the Lion's Mane?

# The Sign of the Four

Published in 1890, Sherlock Holmes and Dr Watson become entangled in a case involving a stolen treasure and a mysterious woman. Their pursuit leads them through the seedy underbelly of Victorian London to a thrilling climax on the high seas.

'How often have I said to you that when you have eliminated the impossible, whatever remains, however improbable, must be the truth?'

Sherlock Holmes to Dr Watson

# Cryptograms and Anagrams

Holmes once observed to Watson, 'I am fairly familiar with all forms of secret writing, and am myself the author of a trifling monograph upon the subject.' Watson, in several of his accounts, made reference to the solving of ciphers and cryptograms. The titles of four of the stories concerned are concealed in the following anagrams.

1   LEAVE US A GRIM TRUTH

2   OR GET A LOST CHIT

3   YET REVEAL HALF OF

4   END CANING THEM

The first four of the anagrams that follow conceal characters, and the next four towns and villages referred to in Holmes's exploits, with clues to assist in solving them.

| | | |
|---|---|---|
| 5 | NAMES HIS LOOT | He was suspicious of three |
| 6 | CAME NEAR TO PIN | She witnessed a violent quarrel |
| 7 | END EARLIER | A successful deceiver |
| 8 | I CRAM THIS DOME | He was master of his craft |
| 9 | WET BULLS RINGED | From where came a bicyclist |
| 10 | SAVE RIMS | A plain place |
| 11 | NOT PULLING LITTER | Scene of a wild goose chase |
| 12 | COME BOY, REACT | Home of L. L. |

# Town Tour

Fourteen towns and villages mentioned in the short stories are concealed in this grid. First find London, then trace your way through the towns and villages. Each word follows a straight line, which may read horizontally, vertically or diagonally, backwards or forwards. The next word always starts from a position that is immediately adjacent to the last letter used. A letter may be used more than once or not at all. Two of the names each have two components, the others just one.

```
A F M D U N D E E L C B
N A A X E U T M K P E N
O R H V R T O W N O P E
T N S G L R L I A S T W
S H R P A C E D A M W S
G A O N T T W E L A H D
N M H R A O T N O H A L
I B O G K T R L N S R A
K S I I O F F H D R R E
S E N J D L B S O A O W
R G C R O Y D O N M W E
R E T S E H C N I W O T
```

# Crossword 4

This crossword puzzle is based on *The Sign of the Four*. Non-cryptic clues, which are the names of characters or places mentioned in the story or a quotation from the recorded sayings of Holmes, are marked with an asterisk.

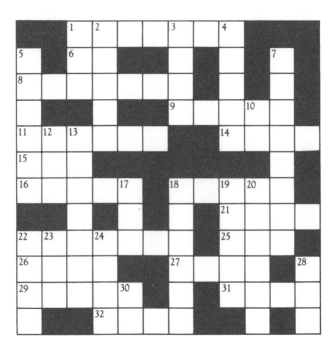

**Across**

1    Ram hens like this to make a bird-stuffer. (7)*

6    A quiet reverse for father. (2)

8    Ben's ale makes it possible. (7)

9    Tendency to tear away after tea. (5)

11   Happy to be behindhand in the small edition. (6)

14   Right away to a disorderly flight. (4)

15,22 Servant who helped dispose of a captain. (3,7)*

16   A boatman who might also be a metal-worker. (5)*

18   Wooden-legged one of four. (5)*

21   'I should never marry myself, lest I ... my judgement.' (4)

22   See 15 across.*

25   'To the trained eye there is as much difference between the black ... of a Trichinopoly and the white fluff of bird's-eye.' (3)*

26   51, nothing else. (4)

27   'a change of work is the ... rest.' (4)*

29   Overturn a minor ailment. (5)

31   She has nothing to make a brave man. (4)

32   Stop like this at the Wigmore Street office. (4)*

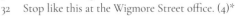

For Down clues please turn over.

## Down

1   Resort to a point before six. (3)
2   'I never guess. It is a shocking ...' (5)*
3   'give me the ... abstruse cryptogram'. (4)*
4   'Women are ... to be entirely trusted.' (5) *
5   'My mind ... at stagnation.' (6)*
7   First name one of four. (8)*
10  Deny in two directions it is snow. (2)
12  Beat the little tailless sheep. (3)
13  Rooms in which Holmes proved to be quite an amateur. (7)*
17  From which a brick might be dropped. (3)
18  Mix bets or make sherbet. (6)
19  Astound, it could be a hit. (5)
20  'If you ... to them under protest, as it were, you are very likely to get what you want.' (6)*
22  'There might have been some credit to be gained out of it but for this too palpable ...' (4)*
23  Take nothing from the hoop-jump! (3)
24  Cry from a wee puir bairn. (4)
28  'I know a ... that would follow that scent to the world's end.' (3)*
30  As far as town but without directions. (2)

# Dancing Men Cipher Puzzle 8

Decode the Dancing Men cipher below to discover the title of a Sherlock Holmes short story. See pages 6–7 for more information on the Dancing Men cipher.

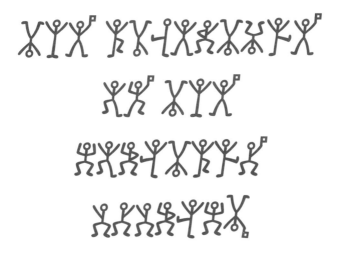

'My mind rebels at stagnation. Give me problems, give me work, give me the most abstruse cryptogram or the most intricate analysis, and I am in my own proper atmosphere.'

*The Sign of the Four*

# Holmes and Women

During 'The Adventure of the Devil's Foot', Holmes remarked to Watson, 'I have never loved.' And in *The Sign of the Four*, he supplied the reason. 'Love is an emotional thing, and whatever is emotional is opposed to that true cold reason which I place above all things.' Holmes as 'the total bachelor' is the picture that clearly emerges from Watson's accounts.

1   However, there was one woman who so attracted Holmes that he always referred to her as 'The Woman'. Who was she?

2   And of whom was it that Holmes said, '... will always remain in my memory as a most complete and remarkable woman?

3   Once indeed Holmes became engaged, although not with any romantic intent. To whom?

The following sayings of Holmes illustrate his attitude to women. Can you complete the quotations?

4   'Women have seldom been an attraction to me,  for my ... has always governed my ...'

5   'I am not a ... admirer of womenkind, as you are aware, Watson.'

6   'Woman's heart and mind are ... puzzles to the male.'

7   'Women are naturally ..., and they like to do their own ...'

8   'And yet the motives of women are so ...'

9  'There are women in whom the love of a lover ... all other loves.'

10 'I have seen too much not to know that the ... of a woman
may be more valuable than the conclusion of an analytical
reasoner.'

11 'It is part of the settled order of ... that such a girl should
have followers.'

12 'Now, Watson, the ... is your department.'

# Aphorisms of Holmes

Holmes had the knack of applying a bright, pithy saying to a situation. Can you supply the missing words in the following quotations?

1   'Where there is no .................... there is no horror.'

2   'There is a strong .................... resemblance about misdeeds.'

3   'When you have eliminated the impossible, whatever remains, ...................., must be the truth.'

4   'It is your ...................., featureless crimes which are really puzzling.'

5   'There is nothing more .................... than an obvious fact.'

6   'Amid the action and reaction of so dense a swarm of humanity, every possible .................... may be expected to take place.'

7   'How often is .................... the mother of truth.'

8   'You see, but you do not ....................'

9  'Life is infinitely .................... than anything which the mind of man could invent.'

10  '.................... is the best antidote to sorrow.'

11  'Only one important thing has happened in the last three days, and that is that ....................'

12  'We must look for consistency. Where there is a want of it we must suspect ....................'

# Dancing Men Cipher Puzzle 9

Decode the Dancing Men cipher below to discover the title of a Sherlock Holmes short story. See pages 6–7 for more information on the Dancing Men cipher.

# Cherchez les femmes

To lead you through this maze are four principal female characters encountered by Holmes in his investigations. Follow these women and you will arrive at the exit from the maze. There are, however, other women hidden in the maze who are not characters in the Holmes stories. If you follow these they will surely lead you astray. All characters consist of one first name and a surname.

| T | R | N | A | S | U | S | A | R | A | H | G | R |
| H | O | N | N | C | U | W | H | I | T | N | Y | E |
| C | A | R | O | L | S | H | I | N | E | N | A | E |
| V | A | R | T | I | M | Y | L | G | L | E | J | N |
| I | S | A | E | N | U | A | L | H | Y | I | N | E |
| N | E | V | R | E | R | R | A | E | L | A | I | S |
| N | C | I | F | N | O | T | S | N | E | R | A | T |
| E | R | O | L | L | U | N | Y | B | I | L | B | R |
| L | E | L | E | T | H | T | E | R | R | N | W | O |
| S | S | A | R | F | Y | R | A | M | E | N | E | D |
| I | E | R | E | O | H | Y | R | A | S | A | L | A |
| E | M | V | L | L | D | E | O | S | I | I | E | V |
| S | Y | I | L | O | N | R | N | P | M | N | S | I |

# Crossword 5

This crossword puzzle is based on *A Study in Scarlet*. Non-cryptic clues, which are the names of characters or places mentioned in the story or a quotation from the recorded sayings of Holmes, are marked with an asterisk.

**Across**

1    Madame, Alice or Sub. (11)*

9    Drink that is in general enjoyed. (3)

10,6 'It is a ... mistake to ... before you have all the evidence.' (7,8)*

11   Change direction north initially for value. (5)

15   Unusual combination of an artist and engineer. (4)

16   Note, seaman makes idle talk. (3)

18,19 Tavern featured in a 'found column'. (5,4)*

20   See 28 across.*

22   Alphabetical extremes lead the little detective to the Central
     American. (5)

24   'A ... in science or any other recognised portal.' (6)*

25   Yes, it's gayer without a little gravity. (3)

26   'The last ... My case is complete.' (4)*

28,20 Ravine where horses waited for two. (5,6)*

29   They were brave enough to cross the desert. (7)*

For Down clues please turn over.

81

**Down**

2   A murderer. With an expectation? (4)*
3   Animal in a crate. (3)
4   Great alkali place for 29 to cross. (5)*
5   Fish back the sheltered side. (3)
6   See 10 across.*
7   Scrawled in blood-red letters. (5)*
8   'The ... of Deduction and Analysis is one which can only be acquired by long and patient study.' (7)*
12  He catches three. (6)
13  Could be shoe, family or forest. (4)
14  Period of the Latter Saints. (3)*
16  Animal sounds not used. (3)
17  A number of persons, or part of just one. (4)
19  See 18 across.*
21  Goad with a sharp instrument. (6)
23  'The most commonplace ... is often the most mysterious.' (5)*
25  Like a relative. (4)
26  A round around a course. (3)
27  Increase the polish. (3)*

# Dancing Men Cipher Puzzle 10

Decode the Dancing Men cipher below to discover the title of a Sherlock Holmes short story. See pages 6–7 for more information on the Dancing Men cipher.

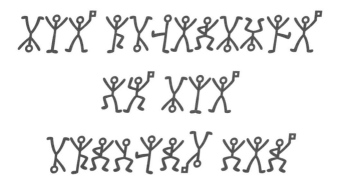

# The Hound of the Baskervilles

Published in 1902, the novel sees Holmes and Watson travelling to Dartmoor to investigate the mysterious death of Sir Charles Baskerville. They encounter eerie legends of a spectral hound haunting the family and confront a deadly foe amid the fog-shrouded moors.

> 'There is nothing more stimulating than a case where everything goes against you.'
>
> Sherlock Holmes

# On the Right Lines

Holmes's investigations frequently took him out of London and railways were the mode of travel of his day. Can you answer the following questions concerning his journeys by rail.

1   Where did the train stop for lunch to be taken in the Boscombe Valley case?

2   At what station did Holmes and Watson alight in Devonshire when investigating the Silver Blaze case?

3   Where did Holmes and Watson change trains in order to elude Moriarty in 'The Final Problem'?

4   To which station did a solitary cyclist ride every Saturday afternoon?

5   What was the local station for the Priory School?

6   To enquire about which sportsman did Holmes and Watson travel from King's Cross to Cambridge?

7   What was the name of the local station for Baskerville Hall?

8   What made Holmes, on a sudden impulse, get out of a train at a suburban station and return to Chislehurst?

9   What made Holmes suspect that the body by the line had fallen from the roof of a train just outside Aldgate station?

10  At what halt-on-demand station did Holmes and Watson alight when investigating the mystery of a charred fragment of human bone?

11  What case were they engaged in when Holmes and Watson travelled with an engineer from Reading to Eyford?

12  What was unusual about Watson's rail journey with a Retired Colourman?

# Medical Matters

As a practising GP, Dr Watson was naturally interested in matters affecting fellow doctors, and duly chronicled their activities. What do you remember of the following, as recorded in Holmes's exploits?

1   What was the name of the village GP who 'had never seen such injuries since the Birlstone railway smash'?

2   Whose house was seen to be on fire from Eyford station in 'The Adventure of the Engineer's Thumb'?

3   How did Dr Percy Trevelyan's resident patient meet his end?

4   Who purchased Dr Watson's practice when he returned to live at Baker Street?

5   Of whom was Dr Barnicot so enthusiastic an admirer that he filled his house with books and pictures of him?

6   Why did Dr Leslie Armstrong lead Holmes a dance in the neighbourhood of Cambridge?

7   Who found 'two brothers laughing and singing and their sister stone dead'?

8   What was the name of the famous surgeon who attended Holmes after the murderous attack on him in 'The Adventure of the Illustrious Client'.

9   What was it that Sir James Saunders was able to diagnose that Mr Kent was not.

10  With whom did Dr Ray Ernest, chess player, elope?

11  What was the name of the surgeon of the penal colony on Blair Island?

12  In what way was Holmes responsible for the death of Dr Grimesby Roylott?

# Matched Doubles

The names in the left-hand column are of characters found in the short stories. Can you match the characters with the appropriate story titles from the right-hand column? The phrase 'The Adventure of' has been omitted from the titles.

| | | | |
|---|---|---|---|
| 1 | Lord Backwater | A | A Scandal in Bohemia |
| 2 | Neville St Clair | B | A Case of Identity |
| 3 | Victor Hatherley | C | The Man with the Twisted Lip |
| 4 | Lord Holdhurst | D | The Blue Carbuncle |
| 5 | John Horner | E | The Engineer's Thumb |
| 6 | Count von Kramm | F | The Noble Bachelor |
| 7 | Harold Latimer | G | The Copper Beeches |
| 8 | Colonel Spence Munro | H | Silver Blaze |
| 9 | Hall Pycroft | I | The Stockbroker's Clerk |
| 10 | Lord St Simon | J | The Musgrave Ritual |
| 11 | Janet Tregellis | K | The Naval Treaty |
| 12 | James Windibank | L | The Greek Interpreter |

# Dancing Men Cipher Puzzle 11

Decode the Dancing Men cipher below to discover the title of a Sherlock Holmes short story. See pages 6–7 for more information on the Dancing Men cipher.

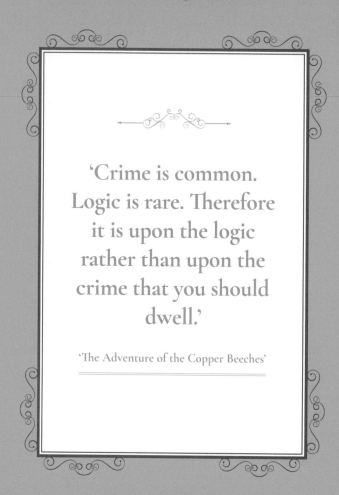

'Crime is common. Logic is rare. Therefore it is upon the logic rather than upon the crime that you should dwell.'

'The Adventure of the Copper Beeches'

# Crossword 6

This crossword is based on the short stories under the title *The Adventures of Sherlock Holmes*. Non-cryptic clues, which are the names of characters or places or a quotation from the sayings of Holmes, are marked with an asterisk.

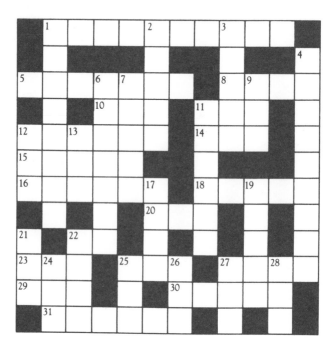

**Across**

1   Mary, she mistook the identity of her lover. (10)*
5   Wooden-legged greengrocer, who should do well. (7)*
8   Make a liar turn to coinage. (4)
10  Trifle with a plaything. (3)
11  Then after tea get the bird. (3)
12  Light meals. (6)
14  Sounds as though the vase could acquire money. (3)
15  An A 1 leg is required to make one nimble. (5)
16  The home of six, near Lee in Kent. (6)
18  'the more bizarre a ... is the less mysterious it proves to be.' (5)*
20  'This looks like one of those unwelcome social summonses
    which call upon a man either to be bored or to ...' (3)*
22,31  Two rands are mixed to make the recordist. (2,6)*
23  Midas reveals the girl in the document. (3)
25  Weapon for a limb. (3)
27  Take a meal back for the girl. (4)
29  Trap set in one tunnel. (3)
30  Alias Windibank, but not from Heaven. (5)*
31  See 22 across.*

For Down clues please turn over.

**95**

## Down

1   'life is infinitely ... than anything which the mind of a man could invent.' (8)*
2   No. 2 armament for dealing with a twister. (5)*
3   See 19 down.*
4   Not Holmes's usual den, but Watson found him there amongst the dregs. (3,2,4)*
6   Beggarly business man. (2,5)*
7   Bent by Dr Roylott, straightened by Holmes. (5)*
9   Alpha in Bloomsbury, Crown at Stoke Moran. (3)*
11  Violet ... consulted Holmes regarding an unusual situation. (6)*
12  In his act one sees a pouch. (3)
13  Help for 23 this way. (3)
17  A slight smear. (4)
19,3 For Holmes she was always THE woman. (5,5)*
21  'the vilest alleys in London do not present a more dreadful record of ... than does the smiling and beautiful countryside.' (3)*
22  'It is a capital mistake to theorize before one has ... (4)*
24  Ed returns to the west to find moisture. (3)
25  Stupid fellow from a German regiment. (3)
26  'when a clever ... turns his brains to crime it is the worst of all.' (3)*
27  Encourage, for example a note. (3)
28  Still unwell following a saint. (3)
26  A round around a course. (3)
27  Increase the polish. (3)*

# Dancing Men Cipher Puzzle 12

Decode the Dancing Men cipher below to discover the title of a Sherlock Holmes short story. See pages 6–7 for more information on the Dancing Men cipher.

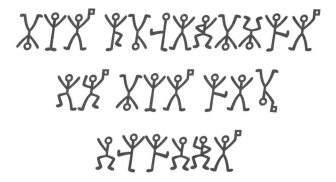

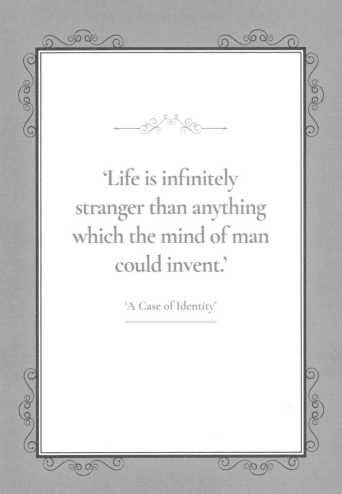

'Life is infinitely stranger than anything which the mind of man could invent.'

'A Case of Identity'

# Watson, the Man

Holmes once observed to Watson, 'You have a grand gift of silence. It makes you quite invaluable as a companion.' Watson, the chronicler, was indeed a faithful and long-suffering companion to Holmes throughout most of the latter's active career. But how much do you know about him?

1   To which regiment was Watson posted when he was appointed as an assistant surgeon in the army?

2   From whom did Watson purchase a medical practice after his marriage?

3   Why did Watson receive such a good price when he eventually sold the practice to Dr Verner?

4   After telling his wife to be of his love, Watson reflected, 'Whoever had lost a treasure, I knew that night I'd gained one.' Who had lost what treasure?

5   For which team had Watson once played rugby?

6   Upon what did Watson say he spent about half his wound pension?

7   What alias did Watson take in the Illustrious Client case?

8   Holmes was famous for his disguises. In 'His Last Bow' Watson too assumes a disguise. As what?

9   Why did Watson once make an intensive study of Chinese pottery?

10  What was the weakness shared by Holmes and Watson that took them to an establishment in Northumberland Avenue?

11  In the Three Garridebs case Watson 'for the one and only time caught a glimpse of a great heart as well as a great brain' in Holmes. What occasioned that?

12  Where did Watson store his papers relating to Holmes's cases?

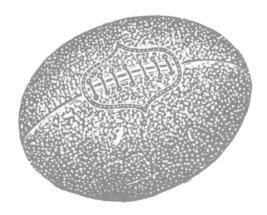

# A. C. D.

We owe it all to the fertile brain and imagination of Sir Arthur Conan Doyle. Here is a quiz about the life of the creator of Sherlock Holmes. Do you know ...

1   ... after whom he was given his second name?

2   ... the name of the paper he edited while at school?

3   ... the first two stories he had published while studying to be a doctor?

4   ... his first medical post?

5   ... the book in which his first Sherlock Holmes story was published?

6   ... the name of the first Sherlock Holmes story to appear in *The Strand Magazine*?

7   ... his pet name for his wife, Louise?

8   ... the first name of his first son?

9   ... the paper to which he was accredited as a war correspondent during the Sudan War of 1896–9?

10  ... the name of the medical unit in which he served during the Boer War?

11 ... when he first 'turned detective' in 1906, the name of the imprisoned person whom he cleared?

12 ... where he was buried?

# *The Valley of Fear*

A murder mystery entwined with a tale of a secret society, this novel, published in 1914 and 1915, centres upon the murder of John Douglas in a remote English manor. Sherlock's investigation uncovers a web of intrigue involving an American criminal organization.

'Everything comes in circles ... The old wheel turns, and the same spoke comes up. It's all been done before, and will be again.'

Sherlock Holmes

# Dancing Men Cipher Puzzle 13

Decode the Dancing Men cipher below to discover the title of a Sherlock Holmes short story. See pages 6–7 for more information on the Dancing Men cipher.

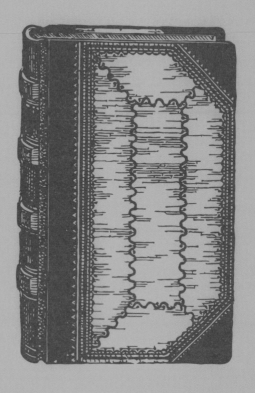

# Stories

# *The Adventures of Sherlock Holmes*

This series of twelve stories was published in serial form from July 1891 to June 1892 and consists of:

'A Scandal in Bohemia'
'The Red-Headed League'
'A Case of Identity'
'The Boscombe Valley Mystery'
'The Five Orange Pips'
'The Man with the Twisted Lip'
'The Adventure of the Blue Carbuncle'
'The Adventure of the Speckled Band'
'The Adventure of the Engineer's Thumb'
'The Adventure of the Noble Bachelor'
'The Adventure of the Beryl Coronet'
'The Adventure of the Copper Beeches'

# *The Memoirs of Sherlock Holmes*

This series of twelve stories was published in serial form from December 1892–July 1902 and consists of:

# *The Return of Sherlock Holmes*

This series of thirteen stories was published from September 1903 to December 1904 and consists of:

'The Adventure of the Empty House'
'The Adventure of the Norwood Builder'
'The Adventure of the Dancing Men'
'The Adventure of the Solitary Cyclist'
'The Adventure of the Priory School'
'The Adventure of Black Peter'
'The Adventure of Charles Augustus Milverton'
'The Adventure of the Six Napoleons'
'The Adventure of the Three Students'
'The Adventure of the Golden Pince-Nez'
'The Adventure of the Missing Three-Quarter'
'The Adventure of the Abbey Grange'
'The Adventure of the Second Stain'

# *His Last Bow*

This series of seven stories was published from September 1908 to September 1917 and consists of:

'The Adventure of Wisteria Lodge'
'The Adventure of the Bruce-Partington Plans'
'The Adventure of the Devil's Foot'
'The Adventure of the Red Circle'
'The Disappearance of Lady Frances Carfax'
'The Adventure of the Dying Detective'
'His Last Bow'

# *Other Short Stories*

Two further titles were written for special occasions.

'The Field Bazaar' in 1896.

'How Watson Learned the Trick' in 1924.

# *The Case-Book of Sherlock Holmes*

This series of twelve stories was first published from October 1921 to April 1927 and consists of:

'The Adventure of the Mazarin Stone'
'The Problem of Thor Bridge'
'The Adventure of the Creeping Man'
'The Adventure of the Sussex Vampire'
'The Adventure of the Three Garridebs'
'The Adventure of the Illustrious Client'
'The Adventure of the Three Gables'
'The Adventure of the Blanched Soldier'
'The Adventure of the Lion's Mane'
'The Adventure of the Retired Colourman'
'The Adventure of the Veiled Lodger'
'The Adventure of Shoscombe Old Place'

# Answers

**Page 14 | FIRST THINGS FIRST**
1. Tobias, 2. Arthur, 3. Lucy, 4. Sebastian, 5. Teddy, 6. Jacob, 7. Teddy, 8. Beryl, 9. John, 10. Athelney, 11. Enoch, 12. Fred.

**Page 15 | DANCING MEN CIPHER PUZZLE 1**
'The Adventure of the Blue Carbuncle'

**Page 16 | STREET WALKER**
Baker Street, Market Square, Audley Court, Mayfield Place, Torquay Terrace, Holland Grove, Lark Hall Lane, Knights Place, Yew Alley.

**Page 18 | CROSSWORD 1**
**Across**
1. Charing Cross, 7. Selden, 8. Goat, 10. Mind, 11. Mire, 12. Lyons, 16. Tap, 18. Tor, 19. Alley, 21. Madam, 22. Laura, 24. Garcia, 25. Devon.

**Down**
2. Hospital, 3. Relief, 4. Need, 5. Region, 6. Shady, 9. On, 13. Yew, 14. Study, 15. Grimpen, 16. Tall, 17. Plough, 20. Years, 21. Mead, 23. Ra. (*The Hound of the Baskervilles*)

**Page 21 | DANCING MEN CIPHER PUZZLE 2**
'The Adventure of the Copper Beeches'

## Page 24 | HOLMES IN DISGUISE

1. 'A Scandal in Bohemia', 2. *The Sign of the Four*, 3. 'The Man with the Twisted Lip', 4. 'The Final Problem', 5. 'The Adventure of the Empty House', 6. 'The Adventure of Charles Augustus Milverton', 7. 'The Disappearance of Lady Frances Carfax', 8. 'His Last Bow', 9. 'The Adventure of the Mazarin Stone', 10. 'A Scandal in Bohemia'.

## Page 26 | DANCING MEN CIPHER PUZZLE 3

'The Adventure of the Stockbroker's Clerk'

## Page 28 | PUB CRAWL

1. The Hereford Arms, 2. A signal light from Helen Stoner, 3. Violet Hunter, 4. Lord Saltire from the Priory School, 5. A gold wedding ring, 6. 'The Adventure of Black Peter', 7. To get a brandy for Lady Trelawney Hope, 8. Scott Eccles waking in an empty house, 9. (a) the port, (b) the linen, 10. 'The Adventure of the Sussex Vampire', 11. Fishermen, 12. Josiah Amberley.

## Page 30 | TITLE SEARCH

Cardboard Box, Case of Identity, Creeping Man, Devil's Foot, *Gloria Scott*, Illustrious Client, Lion's Mane, Naval Treaty, Noble Bachelor, Red Circle, Reigate Puzzle, Solitary Cyclist, Speckled Band, Veiled Lodger, Wisteria Lodge.

## Page 32 | CROSSWORD 2

**Across**

2. Edwards, 5. Lie, 7. Peculiar, 9. Daily, 10. Eagle, 11. Whop, 15. Sods, 17. Herald, 18. Birdy, 19. Data, 20. Adherers, 24. Bell, 25. McGinty.

**Down**

1. Ciphers, 3. Douglas, 4. Read, 6. Ivy, 7. Rather, 11. Which, 12. Order, 13. Pay, 14. Ideas, 16. Detail, 19. Dumb, 21. Dam, 22. Egg, 23. Rat. (*The Valley of Fear*)

## Page 35 | DANCING MEN CIPHER PUZZLE 4

'The Adventure of the Musgrave Ritual'

## Page 40 | READ ALL ABOUT IT

1. In a train en route to Exeter, 2. That his brother had murdered a watchman in the Stockbroker's Clerk case, 3. To trace her missing lover, 4. Sir Charles Baskerville, 5. An advertisement for red-headed men, 6. Colonel Valentine Walter, 7. Bartholomew Sholto, 8. *A Study in Scarlet*, 9. Two human ears, 10. To receive messages from her husband in the agony column, 11. That her marriage would not take place, 12. 'The Adventure of the Retired Colourman'.

## Page 42 | MURDER!

1 – D, 2 – G, 3 – A, 4 – B, 5 – I, 6 – F, 7 – E, 8 – C, 9 – H, 10 – L, 11 – K, 12 – J.

## Page 43 | DANCING MEN CIPHER PUZZLE 5

'The Adventure of the Golden Pince-Nez'

## Page 46 | HOLMES, THE MAN

1. The French artist, Vernet, 2. Chemical Laboratory at Bart's Hospital, 3. Nil, but of sensational literature – immense, 4. Victor Trevor, 5. He had rooms there when he first came up to London, 6. A broker for fifty-five shillings, 7. A loaded hunting crop, 8. He occasionally practised with it indoors, 9. Cigars, 10. A certain gracious lady at Windsor, 11. A solitary plane tree, 12. The Diogenes.

## Page 49 | DANCING MEN CIPHER PUZZLE 6

'The Adventure of the Bruce-Partington Plans'

## Page 52 | CROSSWORD 3

### Across

1. Pycroft, 5. Mane, 7. Mongoose, 8. Ned, 10. Eve, 11. Eric, 12. Ronald, 15. I. E, 16. Tyres, 18. Lessons, 20. Darts, 22. Adair, 24. Not, 25. Three, 26. Age.

**Down**

1. Pinner, 2. Camden, 3. Own, 4. Those, 5. Mystery, 6. Exercise, 9. Evoke, 13. Lion's, 14. Den, 17. Racing, 18. Lodge, 19. Stale, 21. Rat, 23. Roe.

## Page 55 | DANCING MEN CIPHER PUZZLE 7
'The Adventure of Charles Augustus Milverton'

## Page 58 | GOING TO THE DOGS
1. The *Gloria Scott*, 2. By following the scent of creosote, 3. By testing a suspect pill on it, 4. The Professor had taken a serum which changed his personality, 5. He sprayed the wheels with aniseed, 6. His supposed mistress in the carriage was an impostor, 7. Mortimer's curly-haired spaniel, 8. It had been poisoned by the son of the house, 9. The dog did nothing, 10. A faithful Airedale terrier, 11. The nature of the dog reflected the family life.

## Page 62 | CRYPTOGRAMS AND ANAGRAMS
1. The Musgrave Ritual, 2. The *Gloria Scott*, 3. The Valley of Fear, 4. The Dancing Men, 5. Hilton Soames, 6. Patience Moran, 7. Irene Adler, 8. Mordecai Smith, 9. Tunbridge Wells, 10. Vermissa, 11. Little Purlington, 12. Coombe Tracey.

## Page 64 | TOWN TOUR

London, Winchester, Reigate, Woking, Croydon, Marsham, Harrow Weald, Stoke Moran, Ross, Kingston, Farnham, Horsham, Dundee, Lee.

## Page 66 | CROSSWORD 4

### Across

1. Sherman, 6. Pa, 8. Enables, 9. Trend, 11. Elated, 14. Rout, 15. Lal, 16. Smith, 18. Small, 21. Bias, 22. Chowdar, 25. Ash, 26. Lone, 27. Best, 29. Upset, 31. Hero, 32. Post.

### Down

1. Spa, 2. Habit, 3. Most, 4. Never, 5. Rebels, 7. Abdullah, 10. No. 12 Lam, 13. Alisons, 17. Hod, 18. Sorbet, 19. Abash, 20. Listen, 22. Clue, 23. Hop, 24. Weep, 28. Dog, 30. To. (*The Sign of the Four*)

## Page 69 | DANCING MEN CIPHER PUZZLE 8

'The Adventure of the Solitary Cyclist'

## Page 72 | HOLMES AND WOMEN

1. Irene Adler, 2. Maud Bellamy in The Lion's Mane, 3. To Agatha, Charles Milverton's housemaid, 4. Brain, heart, 5. Whole souled, 6. Insoluble, 7. Secretive, secreting, 8. Inscrutable, 9. Extinguishes, 10. Impression, 11. Nature, 12. Fair sex.

**Page 74 | APHORISMS OF HOLMES**

1. Imagination, 2. Family, 3. However improbable,
4. Commonplace, 5. Deceptive, 6. Combination of events,
7. Imagination, 8. Observe, 9. Stranger, 10. Work, 11. Nothing
has happened, 12. Deception.

**Page 76 | DANCING MEN CIPHER PUZZLE 9**

'The Adventure of the Greek Interpreter'

**Page 78 | *CHERCHEZ LES FEMMES***

Susan Cushing, Helen Stoner, Violet Hunter, Mary Holder.

**Page 80 | CROSSWORD 5**

**Across**

1. Charpentier, 9. Ale, 10. Capital, 11. Worth, 15. Rare, 16. Gab,
18. White, 20. Canyon, 22. Aztec, 24. Degree, 25. Aye, 26. Link,
28. Eagle, 29. Pawnees.

**Down**

2. Hope, 3. Rat, 4. Plain, 5. Eel, 6. Theorize, 7. Rache,
8. Science, 12. Ratter, 13. Tree, 14. Day, 16. Gnu, 17. Body,
19. Hart, 21. Needle, 23. Crime, 25. Akin, 26. Lap, 27. Wax.
(*A Study in Scarlet*)

## Page 83 | DANCING MEN CIPHER PUZZLE 10

'The Adventure of the Dancing Men'

## Page 86 | ON THE RIGHT LINES

1. Swindon, 2. Tavistock, 3. Canterbury, 4. Farnham,
5. Mackleton, 6. The Missing Three-Quarter, 7. Coombe
Tracey, 8. The recollection of three wine glasses in the Abbey
Grange case, 9. Here there was a sharp curve and a network
of points, 10. Shoscombe, 11. The Engineer's Thumb, 12. He
travelled third class.

## Page 88 | MEDICAL MATTERS

1. Dr Wood, 2. Dr Becher's, 3. He was hanged by his former
criminal associates, 4. Dr Verner, 5. The Emperor Napoleon,
6. To hide the whereabouts of the Missing Three-Quarter,
7. Dr Richards in the Devil's Foot Case, 8. Sir Leslie Oakshott,
9. The Blanched Soldier was not suffering from leprosy,
10. Mrs Amberley, wife of the Retired Colourman, 11. Dr
Somerton, 12. He roused a snake's anger by striking it in the
Speckled Band case.

## Page 90 | MATCHED DOUBLES

1 – H, 2 – C, 3 – E, 4 – K, 5 – D, 6 – A , 7 – L, 8 – G, 9 – I,
10 – F, 11 – J, 12 – B.

## Page 91 | DANCING MEN CIPHER PUZZLE 11
'The Adventure of the Three Students'

## Page 94 | CROSSWORD 6
**Across**

1. Sutherland, 5. Prosper, 8. Lira, 10. Toy, 11. Hen, 12. Snacks, 14. Um, 15. Agile, 16. Cedars, 18. Thing, 20. Lie, 22. Dr, 23. Ida, 25. Ann, 27. Enid, 29. Net, 30. Angel, 31. Watson.

**Down**

1. Stranger, 2. Eleys, 3. Adler, 4. Bar of Gold, 6. St Clair, 7. Poker, 9. Inn, 11. Hunter, 12. Sac, 13. Aid, 17. Slur, 19. Irene, 21. Sin, 22. Data, 24. Dew, 25. Ass, 26. Man, 27. Egg, 28. Ill.

## Page 97 | DANCING MEN CIPHER PUZZLE 12
'The Adventure of the Red Circle'

## Page 100 | WATSON, THE MAN
1. Fifth Northumberland Fusiliers, 2. Old Mr Farquhar, 3. Holmes had put up the money, 4. Mary Morstan, the Agra treasure, 5. Blackheath, 6. Betting on horses, 7. Dr Hill Barton, 8. A chauffeur, 9. To engage the attention of Baron Gruner in the Illustrious Client case, 10. Turkish baths, 11. Watson had been shot, 12. In the vaults of Cox's Bank at Charing Cross.

**Page 102 | A. C. D.**

1. His grand-uncle, Michael Edward Conan, 2. *The Feldkirch Gazette*, 3. 'The Mystery of Sassa Valley' and 'The American's Tale', 4. Ship's surgeon on the *Hope*, 5. *Beeton's Christmas Annual*, 6. 'A Scandal in Bohemia', 7. Touie, 8. Alleyne, 9. *The Westminster Gazette*, 10. The Langman Hospital, 11. George Edalji, 12. At Windlesham.

**Page 107 | DANCING MEN CIPHER PUZZLE 13**

'His Last Bow'

# Credits

**Images:** Wikimedia Commons: 8, 53; Sidney Paget – 11, 22, 25, 27, 50, 57, 59, 73, 75, 77, 84, 87, 93, 98 ; David Friston – 33; Frank Wiles – 38, 105; Howard Elcock – 41; Richard Gutschmidt – 45; Arthur Twidle – 48; Frederick Townsend – 61, 70; Alfred Gilbert – 106; Pearson Scott Foresman – 19, 35, 67, 81, 95. Dover Books: 12, 29, 30, 47, 62, 78, 89, 101, 103, 108, 114, 116. Shutterstock: Bodor Tivadar– 4, MarGi – 64.

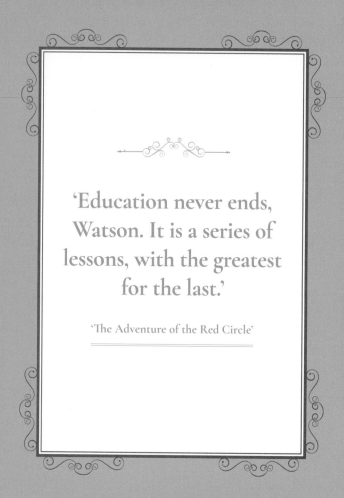

'Education never ends, Watson. It is a series of lessons, with the greatest for the last.'

'The Adventure of the Red Circle'